A Collection of Wonderful Stories
for 8 year old boys:

1 am a 8 year old super boy

(Inspirational Gift Books for Kids)

Table of Contents

Introduction

Hello Super Boy,

Welcome to the book filled with exciting adventures, inspiring tales, and valuable lessons designed especially for young boys like you.

In these pages, you'll meet amazing characters who face different challenges and learn important lessons about believing in themselves, helping

others, and never giving up. You'll discover how the magic of good manners can open doors to new friendships, how teamwork and compromise can solve even the toughest disagreements, and how self-belief can help you achieve your biggest dreams.

Each story is crafted to spark your imagination, boost your confidence, and inspire you to dream big. Whether you're solving problems, exploring new worlds, or helping friends, you'll find that you have the power to make a difference and achieve amazing things.

So, get ready to embark on these wonderful adventures. Put on your thinking cap, grab your courage, and dive into the stories of boys just like you—super boys who are ready to take on the world with confidence, kindness, and big dreams.

Happy reading!

The Day I Became a Hero

It was a sunny afternoon, and Tommy was playing in his backyard. He had his favorite action figures lined up for a big battle when he heard a strange noise coming from the woods behind his house. Tommy's curiosity got the best of him, so he decided to investigate.

As he ventured deeper into the woods, the noises grew louder. Tommy's heart raced with a mix of excitement and a little bit of fear. He walked carefully, making sure not to trip over the roots and rocks on the ground.

Suddenly, Tommy spotted something small and feathery on the ground. It was a baby bird! The poor little bird had fallen out of its nest and was chirping loudly for help. Tommy's heart melted. He knew he had to do something.

"Don't worry, little bird. I'll help you," Tommy whispered softly.

Tommy looked around and saw the nest high up in a tree. He thought about climbing the tree, but it was too high and slippery. He needed a plan. Tommy remembered what his mom always said: "Think with your heart and your mind, and you'll find a way."

Tommy rushed back home and grabbed a few things: a small box, some soft tissues, and his dad's fishing net. He returned to the woods and gently placed the bird in the box, making sure it was comfortable and safe.

Next, Tommy tied the fishing net to a long stick. He carefully placed the box with the bird into the net and began to lift it up to the nest. It wasn't easy. The net wobbled, and Tommy had to be very steady. His arms started to ache, but he didn't give up.

With a lot of effort and determination, Tommy managed to lift the box up to the nest. He slowly tipped the box, and the baby bird hopped into its nest. Tommy's face lit up with joy as he watched the little bird snuggle up to its siblings.

Just then, he heard a gentle rustling. He looked up and saw the mother bird perched on a branch, watching him. It chirped softly, almost as if it was saying "Thank you." Tommy smiled and felt a

warm glow inside. He knew he had done something important.

Tommy ran back home, eager to tell his parents about his adventure. When he finished his story, his mom hugged him tight, and his dad ruffled his hair proudly.

"Tommy, today you became a hero," his dad said with a smile. "You showed kindness, bravery, and clever thinking. We're so proud of you."

Tommy beamed with pride. He realized that being a hero didn't mean having superpowers or wearing a cape. It meant using his heart and mind to help others, no matter how small they were.

That night, as Tommy lay in bed, he thought about the baby bird and the adventure he had. He felt happy and proud. He drifted off to sleep with a big smile on his face, dreaming of all the other ways he could be a hero.

And so, the day Tommy became a hero was just the beginning of many more adventures to come, where he would continue to use his kindness, courage, and big heart to make a difference in the world.

The Treehouse Adventure

Jack was an adventurous 8-year-old boy with a wild imagination. He had short brown hair, bright blue eyes, and a big smile that always made everyone around him feel happy. His favorite place to explore was the old treehouse in the woods behind his house. The treehouse had been there for as

long as Jack could remember, and he liked to imagine all the adventures it had seen. Every time he climbed up the rickety ladder, he felt like he was stepping into a new world.

One day, while playing in the treehouse, Jack noticed something strange. A small, glowing key was hidden under a loose floorboard. Jack's eyes widened with excitement as he picked it up. The key was unlike any he had ever seen before—it shimmered with a magical light.

Jack looked around the treehouse, wondering what the key could unlock. Suddenly, he saw a tiny keyhole in the back wall that he had never noticed before. With a trembling hand, he inserted the key and turned it. The wall began to glow and then, with a soft whooshing sound, it transformed into a magical door.

Jack's heart raced. He took a deep breath, gathered his courage, and stepped through the door. Instantly, he found himself in a completely

different place. The treehouse had transported him to a vibrant, magical forest filled with giant flowers, sparkling streams, and friendly creatures.

As Jack explored this new world, he met a talking squirrel named Nutty. "Welcome to the Magical Forest, Jack!" Nutty squeaked. "We need your help. Our queen, Queen Lila, has been captured by a mischievous troll, and only a brave boy like you can save her."

Jack felt a surge of determination. "I'll help save the queen!" he declared.

Nutty led Jack to the troll's lair, which was a dark, spooky cave at the edge of the forest. Jack's heart pounded, but he knew he couldn't turn back. He remembered all the stories his dad had told him about brave knights and heroes. Jack wanted to be just like them.

As they approached the cave, Jack came up with a plan. "Nutty, can you distract the troll while I sneak in and free Queen Lila?" he asked.

Nutty nodded eagerly. "Leave it to me!"

Nutty scampered into the cave and started chattering loudly, drawing the troll's attention. While the troll chased after Nutty, Jack slipped inside. He found Queen Lila tied up with thick vines. Using his pocket knife, Jack carefully cut through the vines and freed the queen.

"Thank you, brave Jack," Queen Lila said with a warm smile. "You have shown great courage and cleverness."

Suddenly, the troll returned, looking angrier than ever. But before it could do anything, Queen Lila raised her hand and cast a spell, turning the troll into a harmless frog. Jack watched in awe as the queen's magic filled the cave with light.

With the troll defeated, Queen Lila led Jack back to the treehouse door. "You have a heart full of bravery and kindness, Jack. Remember, you are always welcome in the Magical Forest," she said.

Jack stepped through the door and found himself back in the old treehouse. The glowing key was still in his hand. He looked around, wondering if it had all been a dream. But deep down, he knew it was real.

Jack ran home, eager to tell his parents about his incredible adventure. They listened with wide eyes and proud smiles. "Jack, you're a real hero," his mom said, hugging him tight. "And you have the heart of a true adventurer," his dad added.

That night, as Jack lay in bed, he clutched the magical key and dreamed of more adventures. He knew that as long as he had courage and a kind heart, he could face any challenge, whether in the Magical Forest or in his own backyard.

The Magic of Good Manners

Timmy the Turtle was a curious and adventurous turtle with a shiny green shell and bright, inquisitive eyes. He loved exploring the world around him and discovering new things. One sunny afternoon, while wandering through the forest, Timmy stumbled upon a hidden path he had never seen before.

With a mix of excitement and curiosity, Timmy decided to follow the path. It led him to a magical village called Mannerville. The village was enchanting, with houses made of candy, sparkling fountains, and flowers that sang sweet melodies.

As Timmy entered the village, he saw a sign that read, "Welcome to Mannerville, where good manners create magic!" Timmy was intrigued and wondered what that meant. He decided to explore and find out.

The first creature Timmy met was Polly the Parrot, who was busy arranging colorful flowers. "Hello!" Timmy greeted cheerfully.

Polly looked up and smiled. "Good morning! You must be new here. My name is Polly. What's your name?"

"I'm Timmy. I just found this village and it's amazing!" Timmy replied.

Polly nodded. "Welcome, Timmy! In Mannerville, we believe that good manners create magic. When you use polite words like 'please' and 'thank you,' wonderful things happen."

Timmy was curious. "Can you show me?"

"Of course!" Polly said. She handed Timmy a flower and said, "Please hold this for me, Timmy."

As soon as Timmy took the flower and said, "Sure, Polly," the flower began to glow and sparkles filled the air. Timmy's eyes widened with amazement.

"Wow! That's incredible!" Timmy exclaimed.

Polly smiled. "See? Good manners have magical powers here."

Timmy continued exploring Mannerville and met many other friendly creatures. He helped Freddy the Frog carry a basket of fruits and said, "You're welcome," when Freddy thanked him. Instantly, the fruits turned into delicious candies.

Next, Timmy found Lucy the Ladybug struggling to reach a book on a high shelf. "Can I help you?" Timmy asked politely.

"Yes, please," Lucy said with a grateful smile. When Timmy handed her the book, it started to glow and a beautiful rainbow appeared in the sky.

Everywhere Timmy went, he used good manners and saw the magic they created. He realized that being polite and kind not only made others happy but also brought a special kind of magic into his life.

As the sun began to set, Timmy decided it was time to head back home. He thanked all his new friends and made his way to the edge of Mannerville. Just before he left, Polly the Parrot flew over to him.

"Timmy, you've learned the magic of good manners. Remember, being polite and kind will always open doors to new friendships and exciting adventures," Polly said.

Timmy nodded. "Thank you, Polly. I'll never forget what I've learned here."

With a happy heart, Timmy followed the path back to his home. He couldn't wait to share his adventure with his family and friends. That night, as he lay in his cozy bed, Timmy thought about all the magical moments he had experienced. He knew that good manners were more than just polite words—they were a way to bring joy and magic into the world.

And so, Timmy the Turtle's adventure in Mannerville taught him the true power of good manners. From that day on, he made sure to always be polite and kind, knowing that these simple actions could create the most wonderful magic of all.

Safety First - Bobby and the Great Forest Escape

Bobby was an adventurous 8-year-old boy with a head full of curly brown hair and bright, curious eyes. He loved exploring the forest near his house. Every day after school, he would venture into the

woods to discover new things and imagine exciting adventures.

One sunny afternoon, Bobby decided to explore a part of the forest he had never been to before. As he wandered deeper and deeper, he marveled at the tall trees and colorful flowers. He chased butterflies and followed a hopping bunny, losing track of time and direction.

After a while, Bobby realized he didn't recognize his surroundings. The trees looked unfamiliar, and the forest seemed denser. Panic started to creep in. "Oh no, I'm lost!" he whispered to himself, his heart pounding.

Bobby took a deep breath and tried to remember the safety rules his parents had taught him. "Stay calm and think," he told himself. His dad had always said, "If you ever get lost, don't panic. Stay where you are and look for help."

Just then, Bobby heard a soft hooting sound. He looked up and saw a wise old owl perched on a branch. The owl had big, round eyes and a gentle expression. "Hello there, young one," the owl hooted. "You seem to be lost. My name is Oliver, and I can help you find your way home."

Bobby felt a sense of relief wash over him. "Hi, Oliver. I'm Bobby. Yes, I'm lost. Can you really help me?"

Oliver nodded. "Of course, Bobby. But first, we need to follow some important safety rules. Remember, safety first!"

Bobby listened carefully as Oliver gave him advice. "First, stay calm and stay in one place. It's easier for someone to find you if you don't keep moving. Second, use your surroundings to help you. Look for landmarks or paths that might lead you home. And third, always pay attention to signs of help."

Bobby nodded and took a deep breath. He looked around and noticed a small stream nearby. "I remember my dad saying that streams often lead to

bigger rivers, and rivers usually lead to places where people live," Bobby said.

"Very good, Bobby!" Oliver praised. "Let's follow the stream together."

As they walked along the stream, Bobby and Oliver talked about the different animals in the forest and the importance of staying safe. Oliver told Bobby fascinating stories about the forest's history and the creatures that lived there.

After a while, they came to a familiar clearing. Bobby's face lit up with joy. "I know this place! My house is just beyond those trees!" he exclaimed.

Oliver smiled. "You did a great job remembering the safety rules, Bobby. I'm proud of you. Always remember to stay calm, think, and look for help when you need it."

Bobby thanked Oliver for his help and waved goodbye as he ran towards his house. When he reached home, his parents were waiting anxiously

on the porch. They rushed to hug him, relief flooding their faces.

"Bobby, we were so worried!" his mom said, holding him tight.

"I'm sorry, Mom and Dad. I got lost, but I remembered the safety rules you taught me," Bobby explained. "And I met a wise old owl named Oliver who helped me find my way back."

His dad smiled and ruffled his hair. "We're so proud of you for staying calm and using your head, Bobby. Safety always comes first."

That night, as Bobby lay in bed, he thought about his adventure in the forest. He felt proud of himself for remembering the safety rules and staying calm. He also knew that with friends like Oliver and the lessons his parents had taught him, he could face any challenge with confidence.

The Friendship Formula

Dylan was an 8-year-old boy with a smile that could light up any room. But lately, Dylan felt lonely. He had just moved to a new town and didn't know anyone at his new school. Every day, he sat alone during recess, watching other kids play and wishing he could join them.

One sunny afternoon, Dylan decided he wanted to change things. He wanted to make friends but didn't know where to start. That evening, he told his mom how he felt.

"Mom, I really want to make friends, but I'm not sure how," Dylan said, feeling a bit sad.

His mom gave him a warm hug. "Dylan, making friends is like mixing a special potion. It takes a bit of sharing, a lot of cooperating, and a pinch of kindness. Let's call it the Friendship Formula."

Dylan listened carefully as his mom explained. "First, share what you have. It could be your toys, your snacks, or even your time. Second, cooperate with others. Join their games, help out when you can, and always be ready to listen. And finally, sprinkle in kindness. Be nice to everyone and always use kind words."

The next day, Dylan decided to try out the Friendship Formula. At recess, he saw a group of

kids playing soccer. Taking a deep breath, he walked over to them.

"Hi, I'm Dylan. Can I play too?" he asked with a friendly smile.

The kids looked at him and nodded. "Sure, we need another player," said a boy named Max.

Dylan joined the game and did his best to cooperate with his new teammates. He passed the ball, cheered them on, and played by the rules. By the end of recess, he had scored a goal and made the team cheer.

"You're really good at soccer, Dylan," Max said. "Want to play again tomorrow?"

Dylan's heart soared. "I'd love to!"

The next day, Dylan brought extra cookies his mom had baked. During lunch, he saw a boy sitting alone and decided to share his cookies.

"Hi, I'm Dylan. Would you like a cookie?" Dylan asked, holding out the plate.

The boy's eyes lit up. "Thank you! I'm Sam. These cookies are delicious."

As they ate, Dylan and Sam started talking about their favorite books and games. By the end of lunch, they had discovered they both loved adventures and decided to explore the school playground together.

Dylan continued to use the Friendship Formula every day. He shared his art supplies in class, cooperated in group projects, and always used kind words. Soon, he found himself surrounded by new friends.

One day, the teacher announced a class project: building a miniature town out of recycled materials. Dylan and his new friends, Max and Sam, decided to work together. They used their creativity and teamwork to build a colorful town with houses, shops, and even a tiny park.

As they worked, Dylan realized how much fun it was to share ideas and cooperate with friends. When they finished, the teacher praised their project, and everyone admired their work.

That evening, Dylan told his mom all about his new friends and the project. "Mom, the Friendship Formula really works! I've made so many friends, and we have so much fun together."

His mom smiled and hugged him tightly. "I'm so proud of you, Dylan. You've learned that sharing, cooperating, and being kind are the keys to making wonderful friends."

As Dylan lay in bed that night, he felt happy and content. He knew that with the Friendship Formula, he could make friends wherever he went and enjoy exciting adventures with them.

Alex and the Amazing Robot

Alex was an 8-year-old boy who loved building things. His room was filled with LEGO sets, model airplanes, and gadgets he had put together with his dad. But there was one project Alex dreamed of completing more than anything: building a robot.

One Saturday morning, Alex decided it was finally time to tackle his dream project. He gathered all his materials: wires, motors, old toy parts, and a big box of tools. He laid everything out on the garage floor and got to work.

Alex worked all day, assembling the robot piece by piece. But no matter how hard he tried, he couldn't get the robot to move. It just stood there, lifeless. Frustrated, Alex sat down and buried his face in his hands. "I can't do it," he thought. "It's too hard."

Just then, his dad walked in. "Hey, buddy. What's wrong?" he asked, sitting down next to Alex.

"I've been working on this robot all day, but I can't get it to move," Alex said, sighing. "I thought I could do it, but it's too difficult."

His dad smiled and patted him on the back. "Building a robot is a big project, Alex. Sometimes, when we face a tough problem, we need to take a step back and think it through. Let's break it down and solve it piece by piece."

Alex nodded, feeling a little better. Together, they examined the robot. His dad asked him questions about each part, and Alex explained what he had done so far. They discovered that a few wires were connected incorrectly and one of the motors was in the wrong place.

"See, Alex? Sometimes problems seem huge until you break them into smaller parts," his dad said. "Let's fix these mistakes and see what happens."

With renewed energy, Alex and his dad reconnected the wires and repositioned the motor. When they were done, Alex held his breath and flipped the switch. The robot's eyes lit up, and it began to move! It rolled forward, turned, and even waved its arms.

Alex jumped up and down with excitement. "We did it! We solved the problem!"

His dad grinned. "You did it, Alex. You figured out what was wrong and fixed it. That's what problem-

solving is all about—breaking down the problem, thinking it through, and not giving up."

The next day, Alex brought his robot to school for show-and-tell. His classmates were amazed, and his teacher was very impressed. "Wow, Alex! How did you manage to build such an amazing robot?" she asked.

Alex smiled proudly. "It wasn't easy. I faced a lot of problems, but I learned to break them down and solve them one by one. My dad helped me realize that with patience and persistence, I could do it."

His classmates gathered around, asking questions and wanting to learn more. Alex felt a warm glow of pride. Not only had he built his dream robot, but he had also learned an important lesson about problem-solving.

That night, as Alex lay in bed, he thought about the challenges he had faced and how he had overcome them. He knew that whatever problems came his

way in the future, he could handle them with patience, careful thinking, and a never-give-up attitude.

Pete's Creative Corner

Pete was an 8-year-old boy with a lively imagination and a knack for finding fun in everything. He had messy blond hair, bright green eyes, and a big heart. One rainy afternoon, while exploring the attic of his house, Pete stumbled upon an old, dusty box.

Curious, he opened it and found it filled with art supplies—paints, brushes, colored paper, glitter, and markers. Pete's eyes widened with excitement. "This is amazing!" he thought. He carefully carried the box down to his room, eager to start creating.

Pete spread out the supplies on his desk and looked around for inspiration. He decided to invite his friends over to join in the fun. Soon, Max, Sam, and Tommy arrived, each bringing their own ideas and excitement.

"Look what I found!" Pete exclaimed, showing them the box. "Let's make some awesome art together!"

Max grinned. "I love painting! Let's start with that."

Sam nodded. "We can make collages with this colored paper and glitter."

Tommy picked up a marker. "And we can draw cool designs!"

They all got to work, each boy choosing their favorite supplies. Pete decided to paint a picture of a magical forest. He dipped his brush into the paint and let his imagination flow. Trees with rainbow-colored leaves, sparkling streams, and friendly animals came to life on his canvas.

Max painted a beautiful sunset, blending the colors to create a warm, glowing sky. Sam cut out shapes from the colored paper and used glitter to make a shimmering collage of a spaceship. Tommy drew an intricate maze with his markers, challenging his friends to find their way through it.

As they worked, the boys laughed and shared ideas, complimenting each other's creations. "Your forest looks like it's straight out of a fairy tale, Pete," Max said.

"And your sunset is so beautiful, Max," Pete replied. "I feel like I'm there!"

When they finished, they looked around at the colorful, creative mess they had made. Pete's room was filled with paintings, drawings, and crafts. It felt like a magical art gallery.

"This is so much fun," Tommy said. "We should do this every week!"

Sam nodded enthusiastically. "Yeah! We can call it 'Pete's Creative Corner' and make new art projects together."

Pete's heart swelled with happiness. He realized that not only had they created beautiful art, but they had also strengthened their friendship. "I love that idea! Let's make it a tradition," Pete said with a big smile.

That evening, Pete proudly showed his parents the artwork he and his friends had created. His mom admired the paintings and crafts. "These are wonderful, Pete! I can see how much effort and creativity you put into them."

His dad nodded. "You've created something special, Pete. Art is a great way to express yourself and have fun with your friends."

As Pete lay in bed that night, he thought about the day's adventure. He felt proud of the art they had made and grateful for the time spent with his friends. He knew that Pete's Creative Corner would be a place where they could always come together, share their creativity, and have a great time.

Gary the Giraffe
Finds His Confidence

Gary the Giraffe was a young giraffe with long legs, a long neck, and a big heart. He lived in the Savannah with his animal friends. But there was one thing that Gary struggled with—confidence.

Gary was afraid of trying new things because he was worried he might fail.

One sunny morning, Gary's friends, Max the Monkey, Ellie the Elephant, and Benny the Bunny, gathered around him with excitement.

"Hey, Gary! We're going to have a big race today. You should join us!" Max the Monkey said, swinging from a tree branch.

Gary hesitated. "I don't know, Max. What if I trip and fall? I'm not good at running."

Ellie the Elephant smiled kindly. "It's okay, Gary. We're all friends here. We just want to have fun together. You don't have to be the fastest; just give it a try!"

Benny the Bunny hopped up and down. "Yeah, Gary! Come on, it'll be fun!"

Gary took a deep breath and decided to give it a try. "Alright, I'll join the race," he said, feeling a little nervous but also excited.

The friends lined up at the starting line. Max counted down, "Three, two, one, go!" and they all took off. Max was quick and agile, Ellie was strong and steady, and Benny was fast and nimble. Gary ran as best as he could, his long legs moving awkwardly at first. But soon, he found his rhythm.

As they ran, the friends cheered each other on. "You're doing great, Gary!" Ellie shouted. "Keep going!"

Gary's confidence grew with each step. He realized that running wasn't so scary after all. By the time they reached the finish line, Gary was smiling and panting with happiness. He didn't come in first, but he had finished the race, and that was what mattered.

"You did it, Gary!" Max exclaimed. "See? You're amazing!"

Gary beamed. "Thanks, Max. I never thought I could do it, but you guys believed in me. Maybe I can try more new things."

Ellie nodded. "Absolutely, Gary. Confidence comes from believing in yourself and trying, no matter what."

Encouraged by his friends, Gary decided to try more new things. The next day, they all went to the big river for a swim. Gary was nervous because he wasn't a strong swimmer, but he remembered how much fun he had running with his friends.

"I'll give it a try," Gary said, stepping into the water. His friends stayed close, cheering him on as he slowly waded in. Soon, he was splashing and having a great time.

"You're doing it, Gary!" Benny cheered. "You're a natural!"

Gary laughed, feeling the cool water around him. He realized that trying new things wasn't so scary with his friends by his side. He could do amazing things if he just believed in himself.

Over the next few weeks, Gary tried even more new activities. He climbed trees with Max, painted pictures with Ellie, and learned to hop like Benny. Each time, his confidence grew, and he discovered talents he never knew he had.

One evening, as the friends sat together under the stars, Gary felt grateful. "Thanks for helping me find my confidence, everyone. I've learned that trying new things is fun and exciting, especially with friends like you."

Max smiled and wrapped an arm around Gary. "We're proud of you, Gary. You've come a long way. Remember, you can do anything if you believe in yourself."

As Gary lay down to sleep that night, he felt a warm glow of confidence. He knew that with his friends' encouragement and his newfound self-belief, he could face any challenge and discover more amazing things about himself.

Greg Learning Gratitude

Greg was an 8-year-old boy with a bright smile, a head full of curly black hair, and a heart full of dreams. He loved playing soccer and reading adventure books. But sometimes, Greg forgot to appreciate the good things in his life. He often wished for more toys, more treats, and more fun.

One day, Greg's grandpa came to visit. Grandpa was wise and always had interesting stories to tell. He noticed that Greg seemed a bit grumpy and restless.

"What's bothering you, Greg?" Grandpa asked, sitting down beside him.

"I just wish I had more cool stuff, Grandpa. My friends have the latest video games and the biggest LEGO sets. I feel like I don't have enough," Greg admitted.

Grandpa nodded thoughtfully. "I understand, Greg. But sometimes, we forget to appreciate what we already have. Let me tell you a story about the magic of gratitude."

Greg loved Grandpa's stories, so he listened carefully.

"Once upon a time, in a small village, there was a boy named Leo. Leo always wanted more—more toys, more treats, more everything. He never felt

44

satisfied. One day, an old woman visited the village. She was known for her wisdom and magical powers. She saw Leo and decided to teach him a lesson about gratitude."

Grandpa paused, making sure Greg was listening closely. Then he continued, "The old woman gave Leo a special pair of glasses. 'These are gratitude glasses,' she said. 'Wear them, and you will see the world differently.' Leo put on the glasses and was amazed. Everything looked brighter and more beautiful. He saw the warmth of his cozy home, the joy of playing with his friends, and the love of his family. He realized how much he already had to be thankful for."

Greg's eyes widened. "Did the glasses really change everything, Grandpa?"

Grandpa smiled. "In a way, yes. The glasses helped Leo see what he had been missing—the beauty of appreciating what he already had. Gratitude isn't

about having more; it's about valuing what you have."

The story made Greg think. Later that day, he decided to try looking at his own life with "gratitude glasses." He walked around his house and noticed things he had never paid much attention to before. He saw his favorite soccer ball, his collection of books, and the drawings he had made and hung on the walls. He realized how lucky he was to have these things.

When Greg went outside to play, he saw his friends playing soccer. He joined them with a big smile, feeling grateful for the fun times they shared. "Hey guys, thanks for always being there to play with me," Greg said.

His friends looked surprised but happy. "You're welcome, Greg! We always have a blast with you," Max replied.

That evening, Greg sat down with his family for dinner. He looked at the delicious food his mom had made and felt a warm feeling in his heart. "Thanks for making such a great dinner, Mom," he said sincerely.

His mom smiled, touched by his words. "You're welcome, Greg. I'm glad you like it."

As the days went by, Greg continued to practice gratitude. He thanked his teacher for helping him with a difficult math problem, appreciated the sunny weather for playing outside, and even thanked his little sister for sharing her crayons.

Greg noticed that the more he focused on gratitude, the happier he felt. He realized that appreciating what he had made his life richer and more joyful. One day, Grandpa asked him how he was feeling.

"I feel great, Grandpa! Your story really helped me. I've been wearing my 'gratitude glasses' and I see so many wonderful things in my life now," Greg said.

Grandpa hugged him proudly. "I'm glad, Greg. Remember, gratitude is a powerful thing. It can turn what we have into enough and make us happier."

That night, as Greg lay in bed, he thought about all the good things in his life. He felt grateful for his family, his friends, and all the fun things he got to do. He knew that with gratitude, he could find happiness in the simplest things.

The Cave of Courage

Ethan was an 8-year-old boy with a passion for adventure. He was known for his twinkling blue eyes and fearless spirit. Ethan loved immersing himself in stories about knights, superheroes, and explorers, always imagining that true bravery meant fighting dragons, saving cities, or discovering hidden treasures.

One afternoon, Ethan's school organized a field trip to the nearby nature reserve. The students were excited about the hike and the chance to see different animals and plants. But there was one student who wasn't excited at all—Liam. Liam was shy, small for his age, and often scared of new things. He was afraid of the dark, loud noises, and being alone.

As the class started their hike, Ethan noticed Liam lagging behind, looking nervous. Ethan remembered the stories of brave heroes who always helped those in need. He decided to walk with Liam.

"Hey, Liam," Ethan said with a smile. "Want to walk with me?"

Liam looked relieved. "Thanks, Ethan. I'm just a little scared of getting lost."

Ethan nodded. "Don't worry. We'll stick together. Brave heroes always help their friends."

As they walked, the class reached a small cave. The teacher explained that they could go inside and explore for a bit. Most of the kids were excited, but Liam's face turned pale.

"It's dark in there," Liam whispered, trembling.

Ethan could see how scared Liam was. He took a deep breath, remembering that true bravery wasn't just about facing his own fears, but helping others face theirs too. "It's okay, Liam. I'll go with you. We'll hold hands and use our flashlights. Together, we can be brave."

Liam hesitated, but Ethan's calm and confident voice gave him courage. Holding hands tightly, they stepped into the cave. The darkness was intimidating at first, but Ethan kept talking to Liam, pointing out the cool rock formations and the tiny bats hanging from the ceiling.

"Look, Liam! Those bats are sleeping. Isn't that amazing?" Ethan said, shining his flashlight on the little creatures.

Liam's fear slowly faded as he focused on Ethan's voice and the fascinating sights. "Yeah, they're really interesting," he admitted, a small smile appearing on his face.

After exploring the cave, they emerged into the daylight. Liam looked at Ethan with gratitude. "Thanks, Ethan. I couldn't have done it without you."

Ethan smiled back. "You were really brave, Liam. True bravery isn't just about not being scared. It's about facing your fears and helping others face theirs too."

As they continued their hike, Ethan saw more opportunities to show what true bravery meant. When a classmate tripped and hurt her knee, Ethan was the first to help her up and comfort her. When they encountered a snake on the trail, Ethan calmly led his friends around it, showing them there was nothing to fear if they stayed calm and careful.

At the end of the hike, the teacher gathered the students and praised their teamwork and courage. "Today, you all showed great bravery," she said. "Especially Ethan, who helped Liam and others face their fears. That's what true bravery is all about—being there for each other and staying strong together."

Ethan felt a warm glow of pride. He realized that being brave wasn't just about the big, dramatic moments, but also about the small, everyday acts of kindness and support.

That night, as Ethan lay in bed, he thought about the day's adventures. He knew that he didn't need to fight dragons or save cities to be a hero. True bravery was in helping others, facing fears together, and showing kindness and compassion.

Ben and the Art Project Dilemma

In the vibrant town of Sunnyvale, there was a cozy elementary school called Sunshine Elementary. The school was known for its beautiful gardens, friendly teachers, and a big, bright art room where Ben and his classmates loved to create. Ben was an

8-year-old boy with a love for painting and drawing, always carrying his sketchbook wherever he went.

One sunny afternoon, Ms. Parker, their art teacher, announced a big group project. The class was to create a giant mural that would be displayed in the school hallway. Everyone was excited, and Ms. Parker divided the class into small groups, each with a part of the mural to complete.

Ben was grouped with his friends Emma and Jack. They were thrilled to work together but soon ran into a problem. Each had a different idea for their section of the mural.

"I think we should paint a jungle with lots of animals," Emma suggested, her eyes sparkling with excitement.

"But I want to paint a city with tall buildings and cars," Jack argued, crossing his arms.

Ben had his own idea too. "I thought we could paint an underwater scene with colorful fish and coral reefs," he said.

The disagreement grew as Emma, Jack, and Ben each insisted on their idea. Their voices got louder, and their frustration grew.

Seeing the tension, Ms. Parker approached the group. "What seems to be the problem, everyone?"

"We can't decide what to paint," Ben explained, feeling a bit helpless.

Ms. Parker smiled gently. "Why don't you try to find a way to combine your ideas? Sometimes the best art comes from collaboration and compromise."

The trio looked at each other, realizing Ms. Parker was right. They decided to sit down and brainstorm how to blend their ideas into one amazing mural.

"Maybe we can divide our section into three parts," Emma suggested. "Each part can represent our ideas."

"That's a great start," Ben agreed. "But what if we make it even more interesting by blending the parts together?"

Jack's eyes lit up. "We could paint the jungle at the top, the city in the middle, and the underwater scene at the bottom. And we can add elements that connect them, like vines from the jungle reaching down into the city and buildings that extend underwater."

Excited by the new plan, they quickly got to work. Emma painted lush green jungles with playful monkeys and colorful birds. Jack added tall skyscrapers and bustling streets. Ben created a vibrant underwater world with shimmering fish and beautiful coral. They worked together to blend the scenes, making sure the transitions were smooth and creative.

As they painted, they laughed, shared ideas, and helped each other. The mural began to take shape, and it looked incredible. Other students gathered around, admiring their work and cheering them on.

When the mural was complete, Ms. Parker was amazed. "This is fantastic, you three! You found a way to combine your ideas into something beautiful and unique. This mural shows the power of teamwork and compromise."

Ben, Emma, and Jack felt proud of what they had accomplished. They realized that by listening to each other and working together, they had created something far better than they could have done alone.

That evening, Ben told his parents about the project. "We had a disagreement, but we solved it by combining our ideas. It turned out great!"

His dad smiled. "I'm proud of you, Ben. Finding a way to work together and compromise is an important skill."

As Ben lay in bed that night, he thought about the mural and how they had turned a disagreement into an opportunity for creativity and collaboration. He knew that working together and finding common ground made everything better.

Believing in Yourself - Jamie's Big Race

In the charming town of Oakwood, there was a
school named Oakwood Elementary. The school
was famous for its annual Oakwood Field Day, a
day filled with fun activities, games, and races.
Jamie, an 8-year-old boy with bright red hair and

freckles, loved Field Day more than any other school event. He was excited but also nervous because this year, he had signed up for the big race—the 100-meter dash.

Jamie had never won a race before. In fact, he was often one of the last to finish. But this year, he wanted to prove to himself that he could do it. He had been practicing every day after school, running laps around his backyard, timing himself with his dad's stopwatch.

On the morning of Field Day, Jamie woke up early, his heart pounding with excitement and nerves. He put on his favorite sneakers, the ones he believed made him run faster and headed to school. The field was already buzzing with activity, and his friends were all there, ready for the day's events.

As the time for the race approached, Jamie felt butterflies in his stomach. He saw his classmates, including some of the fastest kids in school,

stretching and preparing. Jamie's best friend, Leo, noticed his worried expression and came over.

"You okay, Jamie?" Leo asked.

"I'm just nervous, Leo. I've been practicing so hard, but what if I don't win?" Jamie replied, his voice trembling slightly.

Leo put a hand on Jamie's shoulder. "It's okay to be nervous, but remember, it's not just about winning. It's about doing your best and believing in yourself. You've got this, Jamie!"

Jamie took a deep breath and nodded. He knew Leo was right. He had to believe in himself and give it his all.

The race began, and the runners lined up at the starting line. Jamie's heart was racing, but he reminded himself of all the practice he had put in. The whistle blew, and they were off! Jamie focused on his breathing and his stride, just like he had practiced. He could hear the cheers of his

classmates and teachers, but he kept his eyes on the finish line.

Halfway through the race, Jamie felt himself falling behind the fastest runners. Doubt started to creep in, but then he remembered Leo's words: "Believe in yourself." He pushed harder, pumping his arms and legs with all his might.

In the final stretch, Jamie saw the finish line getting closer. He heard his dad's voice in his head, cheering him on during their practice runs. He gathered all his strength and sprinted as fast as he could. To his surprise, he began to pass some of the other runners.

With one final burst of energy, Jamie crossed the finish line. He didn't come in first, but he finished in the middle of the pack, a huge improvement from his past races. He was out of breath but filled with a sense of accomplishment.

Leo ran over and high-fived him. "Great job, Jamie! You did it!"

Jamie grinned, feeling proud of himself. "Thanks, Leo. I believed in myself, just like you said."

Their teacher, Ms. Roberts, also came over, smiling warmly. "I'm proud of you, Jamie. You gave it your all and believed in yourself. That's what truly matters."

As Jamie walked home that day, he felt lighter and happier than ever. He realized that believing in himself made all the difference. It wasn't about winning the race; it was about having the courage to try his best and push through his fears.

That night, as Jamie lay in bed, he thought about the race and how he had overcome his doubts. He knew that with self-belief and determination, he could achieve anything he set his mind to.

Conclusion

Dear Boy,

Congratulations on reaching the end of this magnificent book! We hope you enjoyed the adventures and learned valuable lessons from each story.

Through these tales, you've seen how self-belief, courage, and kindness can help you overcome

challenges and make a positive impact on the world around you. Whether it was discovering the magic, solving disagreements with teamwork, or finding the confidence to try new things, you've learned that you have the power to be a hero in your own unique way.

Remember, the qualities that make you a super boy are already inside you. Embrace your dreams, believe in yourself, and never hesitate to help others. Each day is an opportunity to use your creativity, bravery, and kindness to make the world a better place.

As you close this book, take these lessons with you. Continue to dream big, face challenges with a brave heart, and always believe in the incredible person you are. Your adventures are just beginning, and the world is ready for your unique talents and big dreams.

Keep shining, Super Boy!

66

Made in the USA
Monee, IL
14 November 2024

70148362R00039